P9-AFS-633

Over in the Meadow

Illustrated by Jill McDonald

Sung by Susan Reed

Barefoot Books

Step inside a story

Over in the meadow

in the sand in the sun,

Lived a bumpy mother toad
And her little toadie one.
"Wink!" said the mother;
"I wink!" said the one.
So they winked and they blinked
In the sand in the sun.

Over in the meadow

where the sky gleams blue,

Lived a woolly mother sheep
And her little lambies two.
"Bah!" said the mother;
"We bah!" said the two.
So they baahed and they ran
Where the sky gleams blue.

Over in the meadow in a hole in a tree,

Lived a smooth mother robin
And her little robins three.
"Sing!" said the mother;
"We sing!" said the three.
So they sang and they chirped
In a hole in the tree.

Over in the meadow

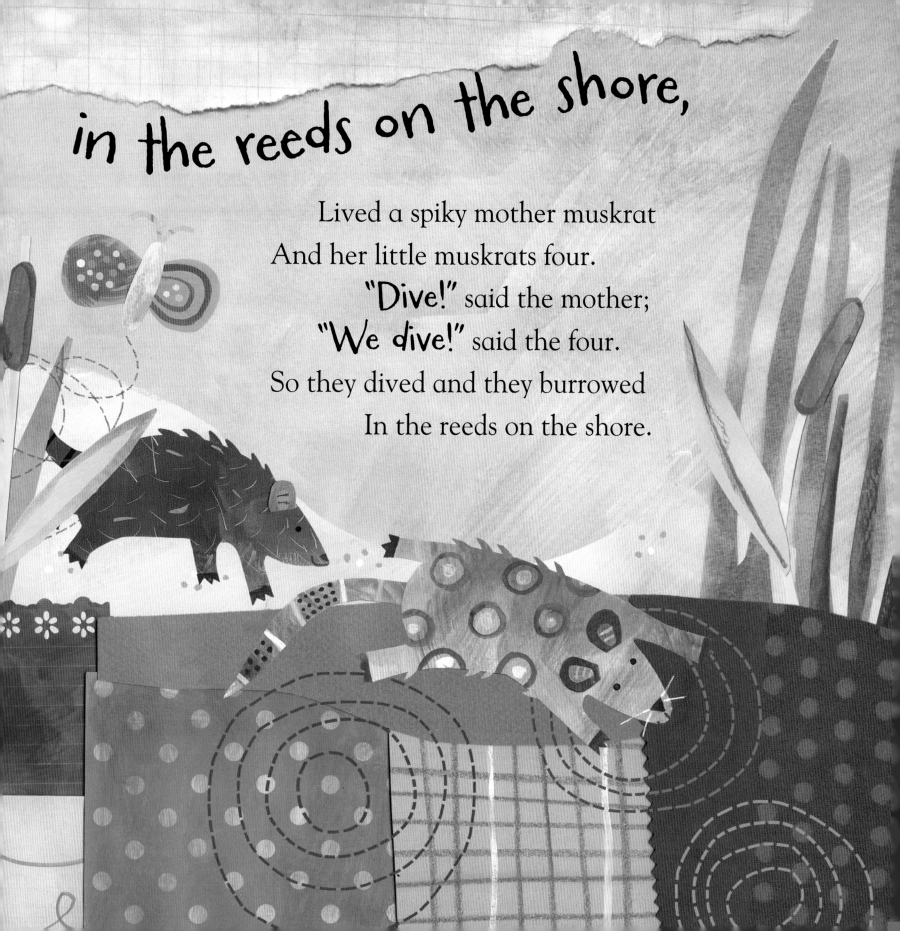

in the reeds on the shore,

Lived a spiky mother muskrat
And her little muskrats four.
"**Dive!**" said the mother;
"**We dive!**" said the four.
So they dived and they burrowed
In the reeds on the shore.

Over in the meadow in a snug beehive,

Lived a fuzzy mother bee
And her little bees five.
"Buzz!" said the mother;
"We buzz!" said the five.
So they buzzed and they hummed
In the snug beehive.

in a nest built of sticks,

Lived a shiny mother crow
And her little crows six.
"Caw!" said the mother;
"We caw!" said the six.
So they cawed and they called
In their nest built of sticks.

Over in the meadow

where the grass is so even,

Lived a furry mother mouse
And her little mousies seven.
"Squeak!" said the mother;
"We squeak!" said the seven.
So they squeaked and they sniffed
In the grass soft and even.

Over in the meadow

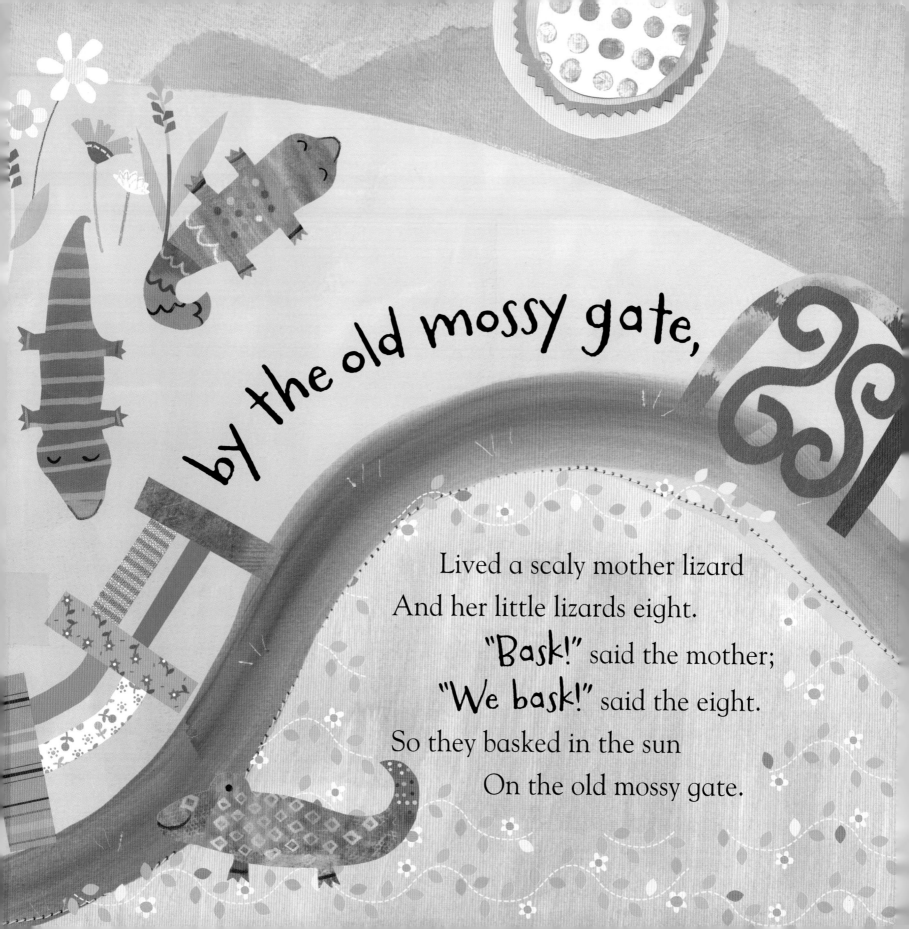

by the old mossy gate,

Lived a scaly mother lizard
And her little lizards eight.
"Bask!" said the mother;
"We bask!" said the eight.
So they basked in the sun
On the old mossy gate.

Over in the meadow

where the stream water shines,

Lived a slippery mother fish
And her little fishes nine.
"Swim!" said the mother;
"We swim!" said the nine.
So they swam and they leapt
Where the stream water shines.

Over in the meadow in a sly little den,

Lived a hairy mother spider
And her little spiders ten.
"Spin!" said the mother;
"We spin!" said the ten.
So they spun lacy webs
In their sly little den.

Meadows and Wildlife

Meadows are a type of grassland. They are found all over the world, from the mountains of Europe to the plains of North America. They contain hundreds of different kinds of grasses and wild flowers.

The meadow in this song is an English meadow. The grass is left to grow tall, then it is harvested as hay. Sheep and cattle are brought in to graze on the newly-mown meadows to fertilize them. They are important homes for many small animals, insects and birds.

Toads live in water and on land. When not swimming in streams or ponds, they dig burrows in the sand or mud to stay cool and moist.

Sheep graze on grasses after the hay harvest. They sleep out in the open, huddled together to keep warm.

Robins use dead grasses, twigs and mud to construct cup-shaped nests for their eggs. They usually build these nests in the bottom half of a tree, on branches hidden by leaves.

Muskrats build dens by burrowing into steep banks along the sides of slow-moving streams. They dig the entrance below water then tunnel upwards, so the chambers inside stay dry.

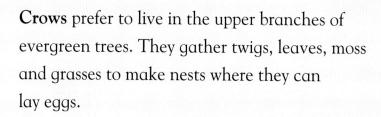

Bees are social insects, living in colonies with hundreds of other bees. Their hives contain honeycomb, which is used for storing honey and raising young bees.

Crows prefer to live in the upper branches of evergreen trees. They gather twigs, leaves, moss and grasses to make nests where they can lay eggs.

Mice nest under logs or rocks or next to plants. They create runways through the grasses so they can run across the meadow while staying hidden from predators.

Lizards are reptiles. To stay warm they bask in sunlight in meadow clearings. When they need to cool down or lay their eggs, they seek shade under rocks and logs.

Fish swim through freshwater streams looking for food. They rest on the stream bed or hide among plants and rocks, but sleep by drifting through the water.

Spiders make their homes by spinning webs out of a silky, sticky thread. They also use their webs for catching insects.

Over in the Meadow

O-ver in the mead-ow in the sand in the sun, Lived a bump-y moth-er toad And her lit-tle toad-ie one.

"Wink!" said the moth-er; "I wink!" said the one. So they winked and they blinked In the sand in the sun.

Barefoot Books • 294 Banbury Road • Oxford, OX2 7ED
Barefoot Books • 2067 Massachusetts Ave • Cambridge, MA 02140

Text adaptation copyright © 2011 by Barefoot Books
Illustrations copyright © 2011 by Jill McDonald
The moral rights of Barefoot Books and Jill McDonald have been asserted
Musical arrangement copyright © by Susan Reed
Music performed by Susan, Kate and Allison Reed
Recorded, mixed and mastered by Eric Kilburn at Wellspring Sound, Acton, MA
Animation by Karrot Animation, London

First published in Great Britain by Barefoot Books, Ltd
and in the United States of America by Barefoot Books, Inc in 2011
This paperback edition first published in 2012
All rights reserved

Graphic design by Penny Lamprell, Lymington, England
Reproduction by B & P International, Hong Kong
Printed in China on 100% acid-free paper
This book was typeset in Carrot Flower and Goudy Children
The illustrations were prepared in painted papers and digital collage

ISBN 978-1-84686-747-7

British Cataloguing-in-Publication Data:
a catalogue record for this book is available from the British Library
Library of Congress Cataloging-in-Publication Data
is available under LCCN 2010041175

7986